We will have to
let him go

Mrs. Bloom stood sobbing by the oven, her body jerking up and down as the tears ran down her rosy cheeks and dropped into the sprouts.

Mr. Bloom put his large plump hands on her shaking shoulders as the sobs got louder. Gently he turned her around to face him and brushed a strand of silver hair away from her wet face. In desperation, she grabbed the front of his old grey jumper and pushed her face into his chest. "I can't bear it," she howled, screwing up his jumper between her fingers. Mr. Bloom gently put his arms around her back and patted her. He sighed loudly, "I am so sorry my dear, but there is no solution to the problem, we will have to let him go."

"The Problem" was laying on his large spongy red velvet cushion by the roaring open fire, looking and feeling utterly dejected. He had only been half listening to the conversation in the kitchen because the flickering flames of the fire had sent him off to dream world and back again, but as his slow realization of the conversation took place, he was becoming more and more awake. How could they even consider sending him away! When they had chosen him, two years before, he was just a ball of black and white fur, a tiny collie puppy. It had been instant love on both sides, and for two years, this magnificent old farmhouse had been Carter's home.

For two years he had lived in the height of luxury. He even had three beds to choose from. The Blooms' bed was there if he got lonely, he had his velvet cushion by the fire in the living room and, best of all, he had a large basket with a warm holey blanket in the kitchen quite near to the oven. He had spent many hours gnawing holes in the blanket in anticipation of the dinner he could smell in the oven nearby.

The menu at the farmhouse was superb. Mrs. Bloom just loved to cook, and the house was always full of the smells of baked scones, meat roasting in the oven and sausages sizzling in the frying pan.

Carter was always given two long walks a day, but would spend a lot of his time sniffing around outside and rolling in the mud. Rolling in the mud was one of his favourite pastimes. This always resulted in a warm soapy bath, a rubdown with a warm towel, and lots of fuss and cuddles.

Life had been good for the last two years, very good indeed, but now all of that was about to change. Because of ill health, the Blooms had to sell up and move into an old people's home and the rules there were strictly "No pets allowed."

"We can take him to the dog rescue kennels at Penton, they'll treat him well there and soon find him somewhere nice to live," boomed Mr. Bloom, trying to sound enthusiastic. Mrs. Bloom nodded slowly, her flushed red cheeks gleaming against her silver-grey perm. "I will miss him terribly."

"So will I, my dear, so will I."

Mr. Bloom's voice had dropped to a whisper as he admitted defeat. He knew he too was going to find it really hard to live without his best friend.

"That'll be £80," growled the tall thin woman with the long black hair. The badge on her blouse said 'Carol Toobad, Manageress'. She thrust a long skinny outstretched hand across the shiny wooden counter and Mr. Bloom slowly placed four crisp new £20 notes into her sweaty palm. Carol snatched the money to her chest and grabbed Carter's lead. "Thank you," said Mr. Bloom, his quiet polite voice contrasting with the snappy aggressive voice of the manageress. "Please do your best for him. Hope you find a good home, old friend, we will miss you terribly." He bent down and gave Carter one last cuddle and then he was gone.

Carter felt a little sad, but not too much, as, always the optimist, he thought, well, it will be just another adventure in life. He tried to feel happy as he looked around at his new surroundings. "Not too bad," he thought. "Choice of all those spanking new fur lined baskets in the corner. Loads of good food stacked on the shelves, really pretty, different coloured leads and diamond studded collars. Real high-class home this will be, oh, and what's that in the corner, by golly there are some rabbits. Wonder what they are doing there, probably tomorrow's dinner, jolly good. Look forward to that, not a bad place all in all, no, not bad at all."

All of a sudden, the glass door to the reception area was flung open and in strode a short muscly woman with bright orange hair and red glasses.

"This 'im, Carol?"

"Yes, new arrival."

Carol didn't look up, her long black greasy hair was hanging like a lampshade over her thin spotty face. She was busy adding up how much money she would get from a litter of puppies that someone was bringing in.

"Moira, take him over the kennels will you, settle him in."

A large rough hand grabbed Carter's collar. "Steady on," thought Carter, as he was dragged through the shiny glass doors of the reception, down the concrete path and across to the dog kennels.

"Doesn't look too vicious or anything. Wonder if he gets on with children, seems a friendly sort of chap."

Carter was stunned. He was sitting on a cold damp floor, and he was shivering. All around him was dogs' wee and poo and the shelves were stocked up with large tins of cat food and a few packets of cheap dried dog food. "Must have some cats here too," he thought. "This cat food cannot surely be to feed the dogs. Well, this room isn't very nice. No warm fire, no television with dog cartoons and the food doesn't look very appetizing."

One of the kennel maids was mashing up dinner in a bowl for one of the dogs and she was actually adding

CATFOOD to the dish. "Right, I will put him in the kennel at the end," Moira shouted, grabbing Carter's collar again.

"Why does she keep dragging me by the collar? I am quite capable of walking," Carter thought, as Moira lifted him up by the collar so far that his two front legs were off the ground and he was made to walk on his back legs. She pulled him into a very small square kennel about the size of the Blooms' bathroom. CRASH went the door and Carter was locked in.

This really was not nice. Small and dark with cold stone walls and just an old grey blanket full of holes. At the side of the blanket were two silver bowls but both were empty. For the first time Carter felt frightened and alone. He put his nose down on his outstretched paws and tried to go to sleep. "Perhaps it's just a nightmare," he thought, "and I will wake up in front of the fire at the Blooms'."

With this thought in his head, he drifted off into a deep sleep.

The first day

A narrow streak of light came shining through the side of the large wooden door and Carter knew it was morning. Slowly he pulled himself up from his old grey blanket and peered out of the wire mesh front of his kennel. Opposite him was a very fat, grey and black bottom. The writing on the front of his kennel said 'German Shepherd'. Carter thought, "This is England, and he doesn't look much like a shepherd to me."

'DANNY', the sign said, and Carter decided that he would speak to him. "Morning Danny, nice sunny one I hope." Danny twitched his bottom and didn't answer. Carter thought perhaps he hadn't heard him properly, so he shouted a lot louder, "Morning Danny, sunny one I hope." With that, Danny spun his head round. "There's no need to shout, I am not deaf, and no, it's not a sunny one, not in here it's not. It's always *not* a good morning, so don't bother asking, and I wish I was dead." Carter was a bit taken aback. Not used to this sort of pessimism and always one to try and make the best of a situation, he said, "Well, try to look on the bright side of life" and then broke into the song, "*Always look on the bright side of life, do do, do do, do do do do do do.*" Danny responded by sighing and putting his weary head down on his paws, ready to go back to sleep, but this wasn't going to be possible as the other dogs had woken up to Carter's singing and decided to sing too. "*Always look on the bright side of life*" they chorused, getting louder and louder until the noise level in the kennels was deafening.

Outside, Stacey, one of the kennel maids, a short woman with curly black hair and a strong Irish accent, had just arrived at work and was making her way to the kennels when she heard the sound of 60 dogs howling together. The noise was horrendous and Stacey put on her earmuffs. She banged the door open and marched in, the noise abruptly stopped and was replaced by repeated barking as all the dogs started asking for their breakfast. Stacey ignored them and walked straight to Danny's kennel where he was laid with his paws covering his ears. "Oh, Danny boy, have you been howling and setting everyone off again?"

"No, I haven't. It's that idiot happy twit opposite me. Why do I get the blame for everything?"

But Stacey didn't believe him. "Oh, Danny boy, try and cheer up." With that, the dogs started singing "*Oh Danny Boy, the pipes the pipes are calling*", but all Stacey heard was howling.

"Right, I have had enough," she said, and grabbed Danny by the collar. "Get up, you can be in an outside run where you won't cause so much trouble."

"But I am trying to get a bit of shut-eye," moaned Danny, shuffling his large bottom across the cold cement floor.

"Up you get!"

Danny felt himself rising upwards as Stacey pulled his collar up. She dragged him into a large run outside and into the warm morning sunshine.

"There, that will do you good." Danny didn't answer and just had a fixed stare on his face as he pooed in the corner.

"Oh, now look what you have done, the morning has hardly started and you're causing trouble already."

"Well, you should have let me sleep," muttered Danny as he sat in his water bowl to wash off his bum.

Carter was shuffling from one front leg to another, waiting to be taken out, but it wasn't his turn. "Not enough runs ole boy," muttered the brown square dog in the next run to Carter. Carter looked at the sign on his kennel, it read 'Boxer' (BORIS). Carter didn't think he looked much like he had been in a boxing ring apart from the fact that his face was squashed in.

"Excuse me," said Carter, "why am I in here and what are all these other dogs doing in here? It's a funny sort of a home, no television, no warm fire, no nice people to feed us sausages and chicken."

"You haven't got a home ole bean," said Boris, rather tactlessly. "This is where you stay until they find you one."

"Well, how does that happen?" asked Carter, shaking bits of grey blanket from out of his paws.

"Well," said Boris, putting a square brown paw to his chin, "what happens, you see, is that lots of families with lots of children come up here every day and they walk up and down looking at all of us. The children poke their fingers in the mesh wire and try to poke you in the eye, and if you bite them the children cry, and their parents say you are a dangerous dog and walk off. But if you stand on your back legs like this," and with that Boris leant back and stood on his hind legs, doing a wonderful balancing act and then finished it off with a pirouette, "and then look at them all sort of pitiful like this and hold up one paw, they decide you will make a nice family pet and take you home."

"Oh right, thanks," said Carter and began practising his pirouettes. "Sounds easy enough," he thought, "easy peasy. In fact, this is not going to be a problem, I will be homed quicker than you can say 'What's for dinner?'"

That day, Carter performed all day while people walked by. He danced, he sang, he looked sad, he did everything Boris had told him to and more, but nobody showed any interest in him – everyone just walked on by. "What am I doing wrong?" he asked Boris. "Well, the sign on your door reads 'under assessment', old chap."

"I am not an old chap!" exclaimed Carter, looking hurt.

"No, they haven't written 'ole chap', that's just the way I talk," said Boris. "If you are under assessment, it means you can't go to a home until they decide that you are fit to go to one."

"How am I assessed?" said Carter, looking fed up.

"Well," said Boris, stroking his jaw with his paw again, "a lady comes up to you and pretends to be nice, but then she suddenly peers at you frighteningly through the mesh and then lunges towards you and scares the hairs off the back of your head, but you mustn't respond. You must not lunge back at her – you must just sit and look pitiful. Then she waits until it's dinnertime and just when you are about to take the first morsel of food, that you have been waiting for all afternoon, she grabs the bowl from under your nose, and you must not object in any way to her taking it. Finally, she pokes you with a long sharp object."

"Sounds blooming unfair to me," said Carter.

"Well, life isn't fair ole boy, that's the name of the game. Stick to the rules and you will win in the end."

Carter's assessment didn't go too well. He didn't like being lunged at, poked at and frightened, but worst of all was having his dinner taken away just when he was about to eat it, but he remembered what Boris had told him because he desperately wanted a home, where he would be loved. Although he had only been in the kennels for five days, he was desperately missing the roast chicken dinner he was used to having at the Blooms' house. He was getting really fed up with the diet in the kennels – dry dog food in the morning and dry dog food at night. Sometimes mixed with cat food. Occasionally, as a treat, some volunteer dog walkers would bring him some sausages, but he just about got the taste of one and then they would walk off. There just weren't enough sausages to go around 60 dogs. He missed Mrs. Bloom's cooking so much. The smells that used to start up early in the Blooms' kitchen when Mrs. Bloom would cook breakfast of egg, bacon and sausages, and Carter would always be thrown some titbits. Then Carter would join them for dinner which was usually steak and kidney pie or roast chicken. Oh, pictures of roast chicken started racing through his mind again. Poor Carter licked his lips at the wonderful memories and sighed.

A minor problem

"That dog is definitely too fat!" Carter's ears pricked up. "He's not that bad, most of it is probably his thick coat," said Moira.

"No, he's definitely too fat," snapped Carol, staring at the dog-shaped blob on the floor. "Nobody is going to be interested in him looking like that."

Carter peered out of his kennel. Carol was poking Danny's belly with a sharp, broken fingernail. Danny seemed oblivious. He had just come in from a walk which he found utterly exhausting and was lying flat out on the wet muddy floor. His coat was thick with mud and Carter had to admit that he didn't look a pretty sight, with his large pink belly squashed around Carol's finger.

Carol frowned. "We will have to start him on an exercise programme from tomorrow and put him on a light diet."

Danny's ears pricked up. "DIET?" He didn't like that word at all. He had precious little to eat as it was, and so as far as he was concerned, his only pleasure in life was about to be taken away. He rolled on his side, gave a big sigh and laid his head on the floor. "What's the point of going on?" he thought, "Might just as well lay here and die."

"Look at the state of him!" Carol was getting agitated. "Do something about it!" she boomed and marched out of the kennels. Moira ran her rough red hands through her orange hair and glared at the lump on the floor in front of her. Suddenly she jumped up. "Come on Danny, back to your run. We will start tomorrow, it will be fun, you will see." Danny didn't look at all convinced as he shuffled behind her, back to his kennel.

Danny felt depressed. He knew he was fat. He was depressed and fat. He had now been on this so-called light diet for at least two weeks and all that it meant to him was that he was being starved. His day began with a very small bowl of soggy food (the so-called light diet) – it was certainly light! Probably weighed as much as a postage stamp. One mouthful and it was gone. Then, to add insult to injury, he was dragged out of his kennel every morning by Moira, who kept saying "Walkies!" in a very upbeat chirpy voice. "Oh yes, she was very jolly," thought Danny. "Well, it was alright for her. Probably started the morning with toast and marmalade, followed by bacon and eggs." Danny's mouth began to water. Oh, for a plate of crispy bacon! His nose twitched at the thought. Gosh he felt tired. No energy, no food, no point. He flopped down like a large plate of melting jelly.

"Come on Danny, nice walkies."

Moira was certainly trying hard. She tugged at the lead, but Danny was stubborn – no food, no energy, no walk! But Moira was not giving up that easily.

"Come on Danny!" She ran forward and Danny felt his neck jolt as she pulled his collar and dragged him along the gravel. He felt his belly being scratched, which was decidedly uncomfortable, so reluctantly he staggered forward. No sooner was he on his feet when Moira started walking faster. "Steady on," panted Danny as Moira broke into a trot.

"Oh my goodness, I am going to faint," thought Danny, as he saw his paws disappearing beneath him. He was running and he hadn't done that for months, not since he had run after the neighbours' pet rabbit, Frenzie. Frenzie had been put out in the garden for his daily exercise, had managed to dig his way out of his run and was now roaming freely around the garden. Danny had spotted him, and the temptation was just too much. He had chased the poor frightened animal until it was too tired to run, and then, unfortunately for them both, Frenzie had become Danny's lunch. He wished now that he hadn't bothered. As well as being a rather slow, elderly, easily caught rabbit, he had proven to be a tough old piece of meat. Far worse was the fact that this lunch had upset the neighbours so much that they insisted to his owners that Danny went. They just couldn't bear to look at him and so it was that he ended up in the kennels waiting for a new home.

Suddenly, Moira stopped running, as she was panting – she was rather unfit too and she needed a rest. Danny flopped to the ground, puffing, panting and dribbling. No sooner was he down when Moira was up again.

"Up you come, Danny," she squeaked.

"No, I need a rest!" Danny decided he wouldn't budge, but Moira was no pushover.

She yanked him up and dragged him by the collar around the field. It seemed like the journey of a lifetime. Eventually, Danny could see the kennels in sight, and this gave him a sudden burst of energy. He made a desperate bolt for the kennels.

"Oh brilliant!" Moira was ecstatic. "Well done, Danny," and with that he got a dog treat, one tiny morsel, not enough to keep a mouse alive.

"She's mad," thought Danny.

Just as he was entering the kennel, he spotted a full bowl of food in Carter's kennel, and it did look good. Quick as a flash, he pulled free and ran into Carter's kennel, and before Moira could catch him, he had wolfed down the lot. Moira was very cross and marched him into his own kennel. "No dinner tonight, naughty boy!" Danny didn't care. He had a full belly and a very smug look on his face as he settled down for the afternoon. But by teatime Danny was ravenous. All the other dogs were getting dinner and he got none. He sat and looked pitiful as the last of the visitors of the day passed his kennel, hoping for one or two dog treats, but it was no good. He was too fat and just did not look like a hungry dog.

"It's no good ole boy, you are just too fat, and nobody is interested in a fat ole miserable dog," said Boris.

Danny sneered at Boris and thought how tactless he was but at the same time he knew he was right – he was never going to get a home, looking like he did, but he just could not seem to get motivated to do anything about it.

The next day, Moira decided to walk Danny and Carter together. Carter was in front and, of course, Danny dragged behind. "Come on Danny, keep up!" shouted Carter, as Danny stopped for yet another pee. "They want to get you a home, you have been here too long, keep moving and get some fat off." Carter was trying hard, but Danny was busy trying to get down a rabbit hole. Moira stopped. A young couple were walking across the field with their own dog. She was a very pretty dog, with brown and white fur and big brown eyes. Both Carter and Danny's tails started wagging vigorously as the couple approached.

"Hello," said the lady, almost whispering. "Oh, our favourite breed! We have been looking for a German Shepherd to be company for our little dog Bella here." She gently patted the little dog's head. "She gets lonely on her own and we used to have a German Shepherd and..." She stopped as Danny was pushing his nose into her hand to get her attention. "Yes, yes, take me home," thought Danny, as he rubbed his head against the lady's soft gentle hand, looking sneakily towards Bella through her fingers. Bella was edging slowly towards Danny and Danny knew straightaway they were in love. Then the lady stepped back. "But this one is far too fat I'm afraid," she sighed.

"That's fine," said Moira, pushing Danny behind her, almost embarrassed by the sight of him. "Come back in a week or two and we will have another German Shepherd in by then."

"No!" thought Danny, "This isn't fair. I could get slim, just take me home with you, please!" but it was too late. The family were driving off, with Bella staring longingly out of the back window at Danny.

Danny was beside himself. "What am I to do, Carter? My first chance of a damn good home and I've blown it!"

"The answer is staring at you in the mirror," said Carter. "Get slim – it sounds like they are coming back soon, so you might have time to lose the weight."

The next day, Moira couldn't believe the change in Danny. He practically ran out of his kennel to start his walk and didn't drag behind when she walked him round the field. Instead, he trotted at her side. "Oh, well done Danny," she shouted gleefully, throwing him a treat. Each day he seemed to find the walk a bit easier and was even beginning to enjoy it, and he certainly wasn't thinking about food half as much as he was thinking about Bella! One day, as they were returning to the kennel, he caught sight of a very handsome-looking dog in reception. "There's a fine-looking dog," he thought. "I wish I could look like that! What a fit-looking slim dog, with its shiny coat and all bright-eyed."

"Look a bit different now, don't you Danny?" Moira was pointing in the direction of the glass in the doors of the reception. "Yes, it's you, you silly dog, don't you recognize yourself?" Danny thought, "It can't be me. I am fat and ugly." He stared again and slowly walked up to the glass. Then he realized that it really was him.

The following month, the lady with Bella arrived back at the kennels, still keen to find a companion for her pretty little terrier. Of course, once they saw Danny again, they immediately wanted to take him home.

Carter was sorry to see his friend go, but really pleased that Danny had seemed to have cheered up so much. "Bye bye old friend, be good, as we don't want to see you back in here."

"No way," said Danny, "you won't see me again."

But they DID see Danny again.

It was a sad evening when Danny came back into the kennels. He had only been out for a fortnight and as he was led by the collar back into his kennel, he was looking extremely sorry for himself. His head was bowed down, and his tail was hanging low between his back legs. All the other dogs had been playing a guessing game for hours as to the reason why Danny was returning to the kennels. What had he done that was so terribly wrong? Barney, the one-eyed Westland terrier, had reckoned that Danny had chased the family cat, but that was not the reason.

Ben, the gentle Lurcher, said that Danny must have pinched the Sunday chicken, but that was not the reason either. Tigger, the naughty terrier, said that Danny must have left a puddle in the middle of the kitchen floor. The guessing game went on until the terrible tale of woe finally emerged.

Danny had committed the ultimate sin – he had eaten the family's pet minor bird, Bootle. Bootle had been driving Danny mad. He copied everything that everyone said to Danny. He kept saying, "Fetch the ball" and "Sit", and if Danny said, "Shut up!" Bootle repeated that as well. One day, Bootle was let out of his cage for his daily exercise, and he was doing his usual trick of dive-bombing Danny's head. The Fartrees (Bootle's owners) had gone out for a drive with Bella to the local supermarket, leaving Danny alone with Bootle.

Well, he just got too tempted. It was like Frenzie all over again, with the only difference being that Frenzie hadn't irritated Danny the way that Bootle did. The final straw came when Bootle landed on Danny's head shouting, "Down boy, down!" In a second Danny had followed this instruction, with poor Bootle down in his mouth and then down in his stomach.

Mr. and Mrs. Fartree were really upset but tried for a day or two to pretend that the awful thing hadn't happened. They put Danny out in the garden where he wasn't even able to run around with Bella. So, he tried to amuse himself by digging holes, and he dug one under a piece of wood.

Mr. Fartree went into the garden to find Danny running around the garden excitedly with the piece of wood in his mouth and when Mr. Fartree took it off him and looked at it, it had written on it 'In memory of Bootle Fartree' so that didn't go down too well. Then Danny tried to make up for the loss of the bird by making minor bird sounds, but this only seemed to make the couple more upset, and so it was that Danny was brought back to Penton kennels. As he was driven away, he clambered up the back seat of the car to look at Bella through the back window, seeing her big brown eyes fixed sadly on his from the living room window. Their gazes held until the car rounded the corner.

Dog eat hot dog

Carter was in the outside run with Marbles the terrier, again! Marbles was most definitely a terrier (he terrified Carter). Ever since Marbles had arrived at Penton the stupid staff had put them in a run together, thinking they would be friends. "Now, this is Marbles," Stacey said to Carter. Carter had cocked his head on one side and given Marbles a friendly wink, "and this is Carter," said Stacey to Marbles. Marbles' top lip curled back, and he displayed a small but perfectly formed set of pearlies.

"Grrr ruff ruff," went Marbles, and Carter jumped back. Stacey had left them together, convinced they would be friends, but they never were. Day after day, they would be put in the same outside run together and Marbles would sit happily at the side of Carter until the staff had left. Then, once they had gone, he would set upon Carter, nipping and scratching. First it was Carter's tail and then it was his legs. Carter, not being one to pick on something smaller than himself would try and get out of the way, but there was nowhere to run to. Eventually, Marbles would wear himself out and skulk away into the corner where he would sleep for the rest of the afternoon.

Today, something was different. There was great excitement in the kennels. Today was Open Day, and today would at least be different to all the other days. There was loads of food around and plenty of competitions to look forward to. Carter and Marbles were being entered for the mis-match competition. With Carter being so much bigger than Marbles, as Marbles was so tiny, this made them look a comical pair. So, for today at least, they had decided to form a pact to try and get on with each other, as the prize was a very large bag of doggy treats.

Carter's nose began to twitch. "What's that smell?"

Marbles pushed his small brown nose through the wire. "Looks like they have brought in a hot dog van for the Open Day."

Different smells were wafting in the duo's direction. Beefburgers, hot dogs and bacon – this was ecstasy and torture all rolled into one. Next to the hot dog van Carter could see a tea and cake stand, and on display were all his favourite cakes. He could see jam sponges and a very large fruit cake and, oh no, his absolute favourite, coconut macaroons!

The mis-match competition was about to start and so Moira collected both dogs and stood proudly in the arena, with a dog sitting on either side of her, and a very funny pair they looked too.

"I say," said Carter, "have you seen the prize?"

"Where?" said Marbles, walking around in circles.

"Up there," said Carter, staring in the direction of a large bag of dog treats perched on top of a very high wooden table.

"Can't see," said Marbles. He was so small that all he could see was Moira's ankles. "Here, get up on my back," said Carter. Marbles started to climb up Carter's back legs. Gosh this was tempting. A leg just two inches away from his mouth and he desperately wanted to bite it; a tail wagging in his face and he really wanted to swing on it – what an invitation! Nevertheless, he mustered up all his willpower and resisted.

Up he climbed until he was stood up on the top of Carter's back. Ah yes, now he could clearly see the prize and a very fine prize it looked too.

This picture was a sight to see for the spectators. This tiny little dog standing proud on the back of this large collie dog. All of a sudden, the crowd went mad. The noise was deafening as they started clapping and whistling. The noise startled Marbles and he started to stumble. "Hang on just a bit longer," said Carter, excitedly, turning his head around to check that Marbles was still there – "the crowd love it!"

Marbles put his head up to the sky and so did Carter. Marbles showed his teeth in a sort of sneery smile and so did Carter, and, in a final ambitious flourish, both held one paw up in the air. The crowd went crazy!

"I think there is no doubt who the winners of the mis-match competition are!" boomed the voice over the tannoy. "It must be... Carter and Marbles!"

"YES!" shouted Marbles, and completely lost his balance. He desperately tried to regain his composure but could only do so by digging his claws into Carter's neck. "OW,

OW, OW," howled Carter and the crowd clapped again, thinking that Carter was singing.

By this time, Marbles was hanging around the front of Carter's neck by his teeth. Enough was enough. Carter shook himself hard and Marbles dropped to the floor in an undignified heap.

"You'll pay for this," snapped Marbles.

"Never mind that, we've won! Looks like we're going over to claim our prize," said Carter as Moira led the dogs over to the wooden table.

"Oh wonderful," she squeaked. "I will save these for later and then all the dogs can have a treat before bedtime."

"But we won that fair and square. Surely she must be joking," thought Carter, as the treats disappeared inside Moira's pocket.

Marbles and Carter were very fed up.

"Gosh, I'm hungry," said Moira. "Think I will get a hot dog". So, this was to be their reward, and a lot better than cold food – this was warm meat! Both dogs were getting really excited as they approached the hot dog van. Soon they were in the queue and fourth in line and they could see the lady in the van was cooking up beefburgers, hot dogs and bacon. This was absolute bliss! Every time she picked up a beefburger, Carter leaned forward, raising his head and opening his mouth.

"Aaahh, how sweet," said the man in the queue, "he's getting so excited." But Carter was getting desperate.

Every time a piece of bacon or a sausage got passed down towards his nose, it went up again into a roll and was passed to someone in the queue. Marbles was rocking from one leg to another and panting, but Moira seemed oblivious. Eventually it was Moira's turn. "I will have a large egg and bacon roll, with lots of onions." Carter and Marbles waited for her to say, "And a sausage each for the dogs."

But she didn't. "For heaven's sake Marbles," said Carter, "she's not going to get us anything! This is really unfair – come on, let's get our own!"

With that, both dogs lunged forward, and the queue scattered. Moira was in the process of taking her roll from the lady in the van and had loosened her grip on their leads. The dogs grabbed their moment. Up jumped Carter and snatched two pieces of bacon on the way down. Marbles grabbed the bacon off Carter. Up again, and a large sausage dropped on the floor. The people were screaming, and the lady in the van was crouched on the floor of the van, frightened that she would get bitten. Moira made a lunge for their leads, falling to her knees but dropped her roll in the process.

Both dogs went for the roll, but Carter still had the sausage in his mouth and wasn't going to drop that for anyone. Marbles had swallowed his bacon, so he got the roll and they both bolted. Moira was up and running, and soon close on their heels.

The dogs raced towards the meadow, but Moira wasn't fit enough, so she went from a gallop to a trot, to a walk, and finally sat down exhausted. Meanwhile, the naughty duo had reached the end of the meadow. They lay down by the hedge and devoured their catch. "Got some tomato sauce?" asked Carter.

"There's a bit on this roll, swap you for a bit of sausage," said Marbles.

"There you go," said Carter, pushing the piece of sausage towards Marbles. Both dogs smiled at each other.

"Share and share alike, eh?" said Marbles.

By the time Moira got to the dogs all the food was gone and two very good friends were enjoying a nap together in the evening sun.

Meanwhile, Stacey was walking around the crowds with a large tin, trying to collect money for the kennels. In one hand she carried the tin and in the other she clasped a beautiful light tan leather lead, which was attached to a fine studded leather collar, which was attached to a rather overweight brown shiny Staffie dog called Corker. Corker belonged to the owner of the kennels, and he was her pride and joy.

Although Corker was a very pleasant-natured dog who was very obedient and had plenty of personality, he was extremely overweight and didn't really get the sympathy vote from the public.

Stacey was wandering around the car boot sale and Corker was feeling decidedly hot – he was literally crawling behind her on all four paws. Stacey was trying really hard. "Please give money for the poor needy dogs," but Corker just didn't look needy – tired, yes! Hot, yes! But needy, NO WAY! Everyone was just laughing at Stacey and walking away. Corker was huffing and puffing his way from one stall to another, collapsing in a heap in the shade of each stall.

"Please help the hungry dogs," Stacey said as she frantically pulled Corker towards a well-dressed man in a cowboy hat. "You must be joking!" said the man, looking down at Corker in disgust. Corker was now spreadeagled on the ground, looking like a flattened rat.

"This is hopeless," said Stacey to Corker. "Come on, I am going back to get a different dog." Corker looked very relieved. Slowly she made her way back through the crowds, watching Corker's every step. She was quite honestly worried he was going to have a heart attack. Eventually she got him back to Lucy, the owner. "I am just popping off home to get my old mouthorgan out," said Stacey and off she went. Soon she was back at the kennels, where she collected old Max from his kennel. Nothing and no dog looked more pathetic than old Max. He was indeed the tattiest dog you had ever seen. His fur stood up on end and it looked like something had been eating his ears. His tail looked as if he had caught it on a bush and half of it had stayed there, and to top it all, he only had one eye. Stacey stood at the entrance to the field where all the stalls were and began playing sad songs on the mouthorgan. She played 'How Much is That Doggie in the Window' and 'My Dog Needs a Friend.'

Max laid down at her feet – this was turning into a fun day. He was really enjoying the afternoon sunshine and he was getting plenty of sausages from Stacey. The noise from the mouthorgan irritated him to start with, so he had started howling. But then, he noticed that as he howled, people put money in the tin, and every time they put money in the tin, Stacey would say, "Well done Max!" and give him another piece of sausage. This seemed like a good game, so Max howled some more with the mouthorgan, and yet more money kept going into the tin, and even more sausage kept going into his mouth. This went on for over an hour until it was time for the sausage-eating race which Max had been entered for.

Stacey walked Max over to the arena where all the dogs were lined up. The pieces of sausage were placed a yard apart on the ground and a member of staff stood at the end of each line. The winner was going to be the first dog to eat all the sausages and reach the staff member in charge of that dog.

Max sat facing Stacey, his eyes fixed hard on the first sausage in the line. "Come!" shouted Stacey, and so did all the other staff members to their dogs, and all the dogs leapt forward. The crowd were all rooting for the three-legged dog called Tripod, who looked the most pathetic of the lot.

Most of the dogs were going round in circles and didn't seem to have much idea of what they were supposed to do, but Max had got the taste for sausages, having been eating them most of the afternoon. He found the first sausage and gulped it down and then it didn't take him long to work out there was a line of them reaching towards Stacey. He ran forward, gulping each sausage down in turn, until he reached Stacey.

"Good boy!" exclaimed Stacey, rubbing Max's neck. Max was licking his lips and looking very pleased with himself when all of a sudden, he felt a very strange lump in his stomach. Soon after that, he felt a very strange taste in his mouth and before he could say, "Give me the fat chicken!" he was sick all over Stacey's shoes. Up came sausage after sausage and Stacey stood there looking horrified. A voice over the tannoy shouted "Disqualified! I am afraid Max is disqualified as he didn't keep the sausages in his stomach."

Max was lying on the ground looking ill. His paws stretched out in front of him, and his eyes glazed over. He felt something brush past him and turned his head just in time to see Tripod limp over to the sicked-up sausages and eat them!

"Ugh," said Stacey, who had turned a nasty shade of green, "dogs are so disgusting."

But Tripod didn't seem to mind that this was second helpings, so to speak. Then the voice over the tannoy said, "And the winner is… Tripod!" Tripod sat up on his hind legs and waved one paw at the cheering crowd. Max was feeling too sick to care. All he could think about, as Stacey led him back to the kennel, was sleeping for at least twelve hours.

Training time

Carter looked on excitedly as the dogs were taken outside, each one in turn. This was the best time of the day. The dogs were taken out into a large field, let off the lead and were able to run around and enjoy some freedom. Carter couldn't wait for his turn – oh, the wonderful feeling of warm grass beneath his pads, which made life seem worth living, especially when the sun was shining.

Today, though, something was different. Something was wrong. The dogs were coming back into the kennels looking exasperated. Their faces were screwed up as if in mental pain. Carter couldn't bark across at Max to ask him what the problem was as the noise in the kennels was too loud. He grew more anxious by the minute as each dog came in with the same mental anguish written on its face. Carter was waiting for Boris, who had been out for ages. At last, here he was, Moira was bringing him back in. A bead of sweat ran down her pink face as she took the lead off him. Boris looked really fed up. "What is it? Tell me!" Carter practically screamed the words out. "Not good ole boy, she's…" but before Boris had a chance to tell Carter, Moira was grabbing his collar and clipping the lead on. Off they went until they arrived at the paddock. All looked normal there. Nothing untoward in the paddock.

No nasty dogs in there to start a fight, nothing obviously frightening. "Training time!" shouted Moira, and Carter looked around for the train that had arrived on time.

He couldn't see anything. This was different and Carter wasn't sure that he was going to like it. "Here, Carter," she cried. Carter ran in the opposite direction, completely distracted by the feel of the soft grass on is paws and the warm sun on his back.

"Here! Here!" screamed Moira." You stupid dog!"

"Stupid person," thought Carter. "Why is she standing there shouting and waving a ball when she could be running around enjoying the sunshine?" No sooner had he thought this when someone grabbed his neck. It was Moira, pulling him over to the fence. "Now, I want you to fetch this ball," she said, determinedly. The ball flew over Carter's head "I wonder what she's trying to hit?" thought Carter, watching the ball disappear into the distance.

"Fetch! Fetch!" screamed Moira.

"She's in a funny mood this morning," thought Carter, running in the direction of the ball to see what she had aimed for. He stood over the ball, looking to see if there was some reason why it had been thrown in this direction.

Moira was still shouting, "Fetch! Fetch!"

"I wonder what kind of animal that is," thought Carter, looking around, but he couldn't see anything obvious. "Oh well, I think I will take the ball back to her and she can aim for the "Fetch" again." As he ran towards Moira, she kicked the chair over with excitement.

"Good boy! Good boy!" she cried, cuddling Carter around the neck. "Now sit," she shouted, waving a doggy treat in the air. Carter mistook this for "jump" and leapt up and grabbed the titbit.

"No! No!" shouted Moira, pulling it back from his mouth.

"Sit! Sit!" This game was getting boring. Carter ran off around the paddock, deciding that this was much more fun.

"Here! Here!" shouted Moira.

"Cheers to you too," said Carter, which came out as a loud WOOF. Moira was waving a doggy treat in the air again, and this was worth going back for. He was now feeling tired, and Moira was still shouting "Sit!"

"I think I will sit down for a bit," thought Carter, and this seemed to send Moira into a frenzy.

"Well done! Here's your treat!" she cried.

Carter looked at her oddly. "Now, down," she said, pushing the treat between his front paws.

"What on earth is she doing now?" thought Carter. "I'm sure the poor woman's cracking up."

"Down! Down!" shouted Moira, as Carter edged backwards, starting to get rather worried by her abnormal behaviour. "Down, you stupid dog!" Moira was now in a state of high anxiety and as she leant towards Carter, she lost her footing.

Carter jumped back in time to see Moira do the splits and fall arm and shoulder into a pile of dog poo. "Stupid, stupid dog!" she cried.

"Stupid, stupid woman," thought Carter as he was led quickly back to the kennels.

Carter's plan

Carter gazed at the small rubber tube. He was bored. Oh, he was so bored. He had been walking around in circles for hours. Occasionally he chased his own tail but soon found that this made him dizzy. The small rubber tube smelt good, and he soon discovered that hidden inside was meat! This excited him, and he desperately tried to get his nose inside the darned thing.

"Why have they put my food in here, rotten pigs! I will do that to them when I get out of here! See how they like it, hiding their dinner inside a football and then shutting them in a room for hours and leaving them to try and get it out!"

Carter pawed at the tube, but it just moved away from him. He pushed his nose inside and moved it around the pen, and eventually he succeeded in getting out the offering, a very small dog treat. "Wasn't worth the trouble," he thought, but he *had* noticed that an hour of his long boring day had gone by. He decided to bark madly at the new black Labrador sleeping in the next run. He threw himself at the dividing fence.

"Push off," muttered the Labrador, opening one eye. "Can't a fella get a bit of shut-eye?"

"I'm so bored," barked Carter, throwing himself against the fence and stuffing his nose through the wire.

"No good upsetting yourself, it just makes things worse. You will only be classed as a mad one and put down," said the Labrador, pulling the blanket around his head.

"How on earth do they expect us to amuse ourselves all day stuck in here?" moaned Carter, feeling particularly agitated as a large wasp settled on his nose.

"They don't care, so you just have to wait until someone takes you home. Now, give us some peace old fellow, and go and find something to do, there's a good chap."

Carter followed the wasp with his nose as it buzzed around his pen. The wasp gathered speed, so Carter chased it. The wasp went between Carter's legs and back round the other way. "This is quite a good game," thought Carter, as he went this way and that, eventually falling over the tin bath and knocking the water flying.

"Oh drat," he muttered as Moira stomped over exclaiming, "Bad dog! Now I have got to clean up this mess. I am sick of this place!"

"Not as much as I am," thought Carter. "Sorry to wake you from your all-day sleep." Moira grabbed him by the collar and put him back inside his small kennel.

"Punishment ole boy," muttered Boris, who had been put in an hour previous for doing his business in the outside run.

"I can't stand much more of this," said Carter, "I have to get out of here!"

"Yeah, yeah, heard that one before," said Boris, "don't see how," but Carter was already hatching a plan.

Carter's escape

Carter was tired. Tired of the same boring routine in the kennels, tired of performing for the public by looking deliberately sad, only to have them whisper sympathetically, "Oh, poor thing!" and "He looks so miserable!" and then walk on by. He was tired of the constant noise in the kennels, but most of all he was tired of getting no sleep. Every night the dogs were locked up at teatime until the next morning, and if one wasn't barking, another one was snoring. Sometimes they would keep themselves amused by singing and Carter did enjoy that. Carter liked singing. In fact, he had always prided himself on his deep baritone howl. It harmonised perfectly with Boris's high tenor whine when they sang together. At night-time Carter would take the lead with songs such as 'Food Glorious Food' and 'Oh I Do Like to Be Beside the Seaside,' and all the other dogs would join in the chorus.

Today, Stacey had decided to take Carter into the paddock for a run around, but even this was getting boring – same old field day after day with nothing in it but an old trough.

Carter would use this to try to make things more interesting. He would deliberately drop the ball in the deep trough just so that he and Stacey could spend some time (him with his head under water, and her with her arm up to her elbow in water) trying to get the ball out. Occasionally he would try to squash himself into the trough for a bath, but it was too small.

It was always a bit more exciting when one of the other dogs was put in the field next to him, as they were only separated by a wire mesh fence, and they would bark and run up and down the field until they were exhausted. Today, though, it was just him and a couple of old greyhounds in the one field. Carter did chase them around the field a couple of times, but the greyhounds were so much faster than him and he never caught them, so this became boring too.

It seemed all of five minutes when Stacey decided that it was time for him to go back to the kennels. Back into that boring kennel where he had been all night with all that awful noise. Back to the kennels where he couldn't feel the grass under his paws, back to... He just couldn't bear it! Stacey went to clip the lead onto his collar and Carter grabbed his moment. As she opened the gate he bolted.

He started to break into a trot, then a gallop. Faster and faster he ran. He ran past the reception but went by so fast that nobody saw him. Stacey and Moira were screaming and running behind him, but Carter was too fast for them. He ran past the cattery and then past the warehouse. The gap between him and Stacey and Moira was widening all the time. He paused for a moment as he approached the rabbits and nearly stopped for a tasty morsel, but common sense spurred him on. One of his paws was bleeding where he had caught it on a stone, but the will to be free and the thought of not spending another night in the kennels made the pain more bearable.

Soon he was across two fields and the noise of the screaming panicking staff was fading into the distance. He caught sight of the Duck and Pig pub and he knew that if he could get down Muckleberry Lane, he would be home and dry.

He ran and ran and could no longer see the kennels or Stacey and Moira. He must have run for over three hours until he saw a farm and some bales of hay. "That will be comfortable for a while," he thought, "and at least I can have a nice sleep." And so he found a nice cosy corner and curled up and went to sleep, and what a wonderful peaceful sleep it was. No sounds of dogs barking, nothing but sweet dreams.

Carter woke with a start! A loud clucking noise had startled him. He opened one eye, then quickly opened the other, because stood in front of him was a small plump bird. It looked strangely like the meal that the Blooms had cooked and put on a plate for dinner on Sundays. It was a lot like his favourite meal, roast chicken!

"Who are you?" yawned Carter, stretching two muddy paws in front of him, which made all the straw stick to him, so he looked like a scarecrow.

"I am Claudia," said the chicken, "full time caretaker of the animals on Folly Farm."

"But you look just like er, er..." Carter didn't like to say a roast dinner for fear of hurting the chicken's feelings.

"I am a chicken and proud of it!" screeched Claudia, haughtily. "And you are a very scruffy, dirty dog."

"Excuse me," said Carter, obviously offended by the tactlessness of the chicken, "but I have had a lucky escape and I will teach you not to be so rude! We ate the likes of you for dinner when I lived with the Blooms." This brought back happy memories for Carter who looked at the chicken longingly and licked his lips.

"Actually, I quite fancy a bit now."

"No! No!" screeched Claudia, flapping her wings and jumping over Carter's head, much to his astonishment. "That is not a wise thing to do, if you want my help to find a home."

"Well, it would be frightfully helpful if you could," said Carter, not quite knowing whether to treat Claudia as a friend or as today's breakfast.

Claudia seemed to be reading Carter's mind. "I will get you some food if you are hungry," she said, as she ran into the pig pen. Back she came with some bits of apple and some vegetables. Carter looked down, disappointed with the offering.

"What on earth is this?" Carter exclaimed, looking down at the bits of carrot and cabbage leaves.

"This is what we feed the pigs – it keeps them really fat. What's wrong, not up to your liking?"

Carter didn't want to appear too ungrateful. "Well, it's not what I am used to. Could you try and find a bit of meat or a biscuit to go with it please?" he said politely.

Claudia disappeared and reappeared ten minutes later with a biscuit and a sausage. "Ah, this is more like it," said Carter, gulping down the sausage. "Is this what the goats are fed on?"

"No, I had to pinch this from the farm kitchen, and a lot of trouble I would have got into had I been caught. The Lofties are a very nice couple, but they don't take kindly to thieving and they would..." With that Claudia stopped talking and stood wide-eyed, looking past Carter.

"What?" said Carter, but he barely had time to swallow his biscuit when a long skinny hand grabbed his collar and he felt himself being dragged into the farmhouse.

"Look what we got 'ere. Caught 'im gobbling down our food from the kitchen. He must 'ave nicked it when we weren't looking, thieving rascal." Carter sat on the cold kitchen tiles and looked up.

Mr. Lofty was very tall indeed, so he certainly lived up to his name. He had a blue and white checked shirt on with sleeves rolled up. His skinny hairy arms were attached to two long skinny hands, and even longer skinny fingers. His trousers were halfway up his legs because his legs were so long, and he had on an old pair of velvet slippers, with a hole in the toe of one, and the backs trodden down where he couldn't be bothered to slip them on properly. His face was very thin, but kindly. His cheeks were rosy, and his silver-grey hair was slicked back with grease and squashed under his brown cap.

Mrs. Lofty did not live up to her name. She could have only been five-foot two-inches tall, and a bright red flowered apron hung over her large belly. She had a big round face and curly brown hair, and a large red nose. One eye was green, and one was brown, which made it difficult for Carter to focus on her, as he was switching from one eye to the other.

"Looks like a stray, poor ole thing," she said. "I 'aven't 'eard of any of the neighbours losing a dog, must have come miles. I will get 'im some food."

"If ee barks we could keep 'im for a guard dog," said Mr. Lofty.

Carter wagged his tail. "Woof woof," he squeaked.

"It's not very loud," said Mrs. Lofty. "No, that won't do at all."

"WOOF WOOF!" Carter hollered. Mr. and Mrs. Lofty jumped back and fell over one another. "That will do nicely I think!" chortled Mr. Lofty. "Yes, I think we will keep him. You can stay here. You go over there by the fire and get yerself warm and we will find you something nice to eat."

Carter trotted over to the warm white rug by the roaring fire. This was just too good to be true. Soon a bowl of leftover beef stew was placed under his nose. "Oh, a bowl of heaven," thought Carter. Once he had gulped down the last bit of gravy he stretched his legs out in front of him and felt the soft warm rug between his paws. He had done it! He had escaped and found himself a new home and he knew that he would be happy here.

For a moment, he felt guilty as he thought about his friends back in the kennels and thought how nice it would be if they could escape too, but how could he possibly achieve that on his own? "I wish I could help them escape too." Carter spoke the words out loud. He heard a rustling sound and looked up towards the open kitchen window. He could just make out the shape of a Sunday roast and an eye winking at him, and he knew that his new friend was going to be very useful to him in the weeks to come...